I couldn't believe it! Mom was going to California with some bald guy named Dink—what kind of a dumb name is Dink?—and she was leaving me behind. And she was happy!

I felt like I had a knife in my heart. I felt like I was dying.

Where did this Dink person come from? I'd never heard of him before, so she must have just met him.

She's going to California with some bearded stranger, and she's leaving me behind. She's leaving me behind!

"Never get involved with babies, Charlie," Mom always told me. "They mess up your life."

I'd always thought she meant babies in general, little weepy, sniveling kids, the ones you see crabbing in the grocery store. But she hadn't. She'd meant me.

The East Edge Mysteries

.50

THE CASE OF THE
MISSING MELODY

GAYLE ROPER

Chariot Books™
David C. Cook Publishing Co.

Published by Chariot Books,
an imprint of David C. Cook Publishing Co.
David C. Cook Publishing Co., Elgin, Illinois 60120
David C. Cook Publishing Co., Weston, Ontario
Nova Distribution, Ltd., Newton Abbot, England

THE CASE OF THE MISSING MELODY
© 1993 by Gayle G. Roper

Cover illustration by Cindy Webber
Cover design by Helen Lannis
First printing, 1993
Printed in the United States of America
97 96 95 94 93 5 4 3 2 1

Library of Congress Cataloging-in-Publication Data
Roper, Gayle G.
The case of the missing Melody/Gayle Roper
p. cm.—(East Edge mysteries: #4)
Summary: Eleven-year-old Charlie, distraught after the
authorities take her away from her alcoholic mother, has
only begun adjusting to life in a Christian foster home when
her young foster sister is kidnapped.
ISBN 1-55513-702-4
[1. Foster home care—Fiction. 2. Mothers and daughters—
Fiction. 3. Christian life—Fiction. 4. Kidnapping—Fiction. 5.
Mystery and detective stories.] I. Title. II. Series: Roper, Gayle
G. East Edge mysteries: #4
PZ7.R6788Cas   1993
[Fic]—dc20   92-39317
                                                    CIP
                                                    AC

For Trisha

The first thing I heard as I entered the house was a crying baby.

I turned and looked at Mr. Anderson, who was right behind me with my navy-blue suitcase.

"Who's that?" I asked. "There wasn't a baby here before, was there?" Surely my memory wasn't that bad.

He shook his head. "She came to stay with us while you were at camp. Her name's Melody."

I listened to the bawling and said, "I sure don't hear any melody in that noise."

Mr. Anderson grunted. I didn't know whether he agreed, disagreed, or was having trouble with the suitcase.

"Babies scare me," I said. "They're too little."

Mr. Anderson nodded. "They make me nervous

too. But Mrs. Anderson loves them."

"Just so the thing lets me sleep." In fact, I wanted to sleep for a couple of days straight. Camp had been more tiring than I had ever expected.

"Your room's upstairs to the left," Mr. Anderson said. "Remember?"

I remembered all right, but I shrugged as though I didn't. I didn't want to appear too eager or too needy. I climbed the steps feeling dread and relief and lots of guilt. I was afraid.

What if these people didn't like me? What if I failed to meet their standards? What if they thought I was as bad as I thought I was? What if they sent me back to Children's Services and no one ever wanted me again and I had no place to live? Eleven is pretty young to be alone.

I shivered.

Yet I had a feeling of freedom as well. I wasn't responsible for anything. I didn't have to figure out how to get food. I didn't have to figure out where my mom was. I didn't have to worry about being put out of our apartment because we couldn't pay the rent. All I had to do was show up for meals and keep my hands out of Mrs. Anderson's pocketbook.

I guess I felt guilty over my relief. If I had character and backbone, I'd be able to manage life without help from the Andersons or Children's Services or anyone. If I were strong, I could take care of both Mom and myself without help. If I loved her enough, we could make it! If I loved her enough, she'd be well.

I walked into the room that had been given to me for my stay. It was clean and pretty, all rose and cream. Curtains with little rosebuds matched the quilt, and the rug was the same shade as the rosebuds. Two pictures of pink roses hung over the bed, and a watercolor of a garden hung over the bureau. There was a little table with a stool—a vanity, Mrs. Anderson had called it when I first came. A mirror hung over the table, which had a skirt that matched the curtains and the quilt.

"You can sit there and make yourself beautiful," Mrs. Anderson had said.

I hadn't snorted because she seemed serious, but I decided that the woman definitely needed glasses. With wild hair like mine, beauty wasn't even a possibility.

"All I can say," Mom always told me, "is that it's a good thing you're nice. You won't get far on your looks."

Mom was gorgeous, and her looks got her everywhere. She was all blond and pink and cuddly with huge blue eyes that could be either soft and charming or shooting sparks. Men thought she was wonderful, and they often proved it by buying us food and clothes and stuff. But recently her eyes had been bloodshot and her skin pale and pasty. Her energy level had dropped. She ate very little and drank a lot. I saw a program on TV about alcoholics, and I know my mom has become one. She says not.

I love my mom so much it hurts. I don't know if she loves me or not, but she only hits me when she's drunk. And she's always sorry.

"Charlie," she sobs as she tries to wrap her arms around me, "I'm sorry. I didn't mean it. I didn't mean to hurt you."

I used to believe her.

Mr. Anderson put my suitcase on the bed. "I'll just let Mrs. Anderson know we're home," he said and disappeared in the direction of the crying Melody.

There was a pink chair in my new bedroom, all soft and plump with pillows that matched the curtains and quilt and vanity skirt. I plopped into the chair and looked around. This was by far the prettiest room I'd ever had. It was also the neatest, as in tidy-neat, not wonderful-neat. Mom and I tended to be a bit sloppy.

I wondered what Mom would think if she saw this room. She was always saying that we deserved better than we had. I was still in the chair staring at nothing when I heard Mrs. Anderson coming. I stood up as she came into the room.

"Oh, Charlie," she said, smiling widely. "It's so good to have you home. I hope you had a grand time at camp!" And she hugged me.

I didn't know what to do. Should I hug back? I wasn't sure I wanted to. After all, I hadn't asked her to hug me. I wasn't used to it. In the neighborhood where I lived, people yelled more than they hugged. And Mom was always so busy being Mom that she didn't have enough time to hug me.

Mrs. Anderson had hugged me the night I arrived. When I came in the front door with the social worker, she had been right there waiting.

"Charlette," she'd said, "we're so glad you're here!" And she'd grabbed me and hugged me.

I was so surprised I didn't know what to do. I knew I was dirty, my clothes were dirty, and my face was swollen from crying. I wouldn't have hugged me on a bet.

"Call me Charlie," I mumbled into her shoulder. "I hate Charlette."

"Charlie it is," she said cheerfully, releasing me. She appeared not to notice that I had been as cuddly as a stick. "Come on. Let me show you your room."

I was only at the Andersons' two days before they shipped me to Camp Harmony Hill for a week, but Mrs. Anderson had hugged me more in that short time than Mom had in my whole life. And here I was again, five minutes back in the house and already hugged.

A particularly loud wail suddenly echoed down the hall.

"Poor little thing," said Mrs. Anderson. "Come on, Charlie. Come meet Melody."

Before I could decide how to avoid meeting the baby, Mrs. Anderson was out the door. There was nothing I could do but follow or appear incredibly rude.

"Children's Services called Tuesday night and asked us to take her," Mrs. Anderson said over her shoulder. "Her mother had left her all alone for two days. A neighbor reported her constant crying to the police. They found the poor little thing in her crib in dirty diapers, cold and hungry. I think they still haven't found the mother."

Sounded all too familiar to me, but at least

when Mom disappeared I could feed myself. Poor little squawky Melody couldn't. If she had been older, we could have compared how long we'd been left. My longest was a week, and then I ended up here.

Walking into the baby's room was like walking into an ocean. Everything was shimmery blue with a border of seashells around the room and pictures of seashells on the walls and real seashells sitting on the bureau. Even the sheets on the baby's crib were seashore scenes.

Lying in the midst of all this blue was a little red crying machine. Her face was screwed up and her mouth was open and her hands were waving and her feet were kicking. She was so upset that her chin and her voice quavered.

She terrified me.

"Never get involved with babies," Mom always told me. "They mess up your life."

I looked at the squalling Melody and thought that for once Mom might actually be right.

Mrs. Anderson threw a cloth over her shoulder, scooped Melody up, and held her to her shoulder. She patted the baby's back gently, totally unaware that the little thing was an absolute mess.

"Watch it doesn't puke down your back," I warned.

"It's always a risk with babies." Her tone of voice

said it was a risk worth taking. I wasn't so sure.

Suddenly a huge burp erupted.

I blinked and Mrs. Anderson laughed.

"Good girl," she said lowering Melody onto her changing table. "I'm so proud of you."

Proud of her for burping? I bet if I burped like that, she wouldn't be proud of me.

Melody lay there, happily kicking the air. Her tears were gone.

"Charlie, stand here and watch Melody for a second, okay? She has a very bad diaper rash, and I need to get her medicine from the bathroom." Mrs. Anderson bent over Melody. "We don't want you falling off, do we, sweetheart?"

Why do people talk to babies in that gooey, stupid way?

I walked to the changing table and looked at the baby. Now that she wasn't crying, she wasn't so ugly. But she wasn't pretty, either. She had blue eyes and lots of scraggly hair that was black at the ends and blond at the roots, like a lady with a reverse dye job.

"How old is she?" I asked.

"Six months, we think. We're not certain."

I stared at Melody, who stared back. Imagine not knowing how old you were. How would you ever have a birthday?

Suddenly a little hand shot out and grabbed my finger. She still scared me, but I couldn't help it . . . I felt my heart melt.

I lay in bed and stared at the ceiling. It was Sunday morning, and I wondered what I would do to pass all the hours that lay ahead. School didn't start until Wednesday, and in the meantime, I expected to be very bored.

I could watch TV. I liked TV. Or I could count the rosebuds in my curtains. Or I could draw.

The last idea was the best. I love to draw. I don't know if I'm any good or not, but I have fun. I've never shown anyone what I draw, not even Mom. I guess I've always been too afraid she'd treat my art the way she treats my looks.

"Charlie?" Mrs. Anderson knocked softly on my door. "Are you awake?"

"Yeah."

"May I come in?"

"Yeah." After all, it was her house. She could go anywhere she wanted.

She opened my bedroom door and peered in. "Breakfast will be in fifteen minutes."

There was a specific time to eat breakfast? I thought schedules like that were only for camp. "I don't usually eat breakfast," I said.

"At least have a piece of toast," Mrs. Anderson said. "It's a long time until Sunday dinner. Okay?"

"Okay," I said, wondering what had happened to lunch. I'd show up at the breakfast table; I just wouldn't eat.

That's how I kept Mom happy—appearing to do something when I really didn't. "Why don't you dust this place, Charlie?" Mom would say as she stumbled to the sofa from the kitchen.

"Sure, Mom." I'd pick up any handy piece of material—a blouse, a sweater, a sock—and make believe I was dusting the table top.

"You're a good girl, Charlie," she'd say with a vague smile. Then she'd lie down, turn her face to the back cushions, and pass out.

I looked at Mrs. Anderson, who was wearing a pretty pink bathrobe with a band of blue around each sleeve and one around the hem. I bet she never passed out, and I bet she never slugged her kids. I wondered what it was like having a mother who acted like Claire Huxtable.

She was still talking. "We'll leave for Sunday school and church in about forty-five minutes. That should give you plenty of time to shower and dress. Okay?"

"Okay," I said automatically.

Sunday school and church? Sunday school and church?

I shouldn't have been surprised. After all, Shannon, a girl in my cabin at camp, had told me she and Mrs. Anderson went to the same church. Still, I'd never been to Sunday school or church in my whole life, and I didn't want to ruin my perfect record.

Suddenly I felt very nervous. What did you do at Sunday school and church? How should I act? And what should I wear?

At breakfast I ate a piece of toast to make Mrs. Anderson happy. Melody was guzzling anemic-looking strained bananas and some oatmeal that looked like lumpy paste. There was more food on her face than in her dish, but she must have been getting something inside her because she was cooing and gurgling and smiling.

When I got up from the table, Mrs. Anderson

looked at me and smiled. I thought of the lady who used to be in the TV ads, the one who stuck all her clients' fingers in little bowls of dish detergent. Mrs. Anderson had short, light hair just like that lady, and she was a little too heavy but not fat. She smiled a lot, and when she wasn't busy hugging people, she patted them, just like the TV lady.

She reached out and patted me. "Wear whatever you want to, dear," she said. "You'll look lovely no matter what you have on."

Glasses, definitely.

I rode in the back seat with Melody. The kid was all duded up in a yellow sun dress with matching pants. She had on little yellow socks with lace on them and the tiniest black patent leather shoes I'd ever seen.

She kept staring at me and gurgling. I guess she thought she was talking to me. I just hoped she didn't think she was telling me anything important because I certainly had no idea what she was saying.

"Does Melody come from somewhere around here?" I asked.

Mrs. Anderson nodded. "Children's Services is a county agency, so she must come from within the county. I don't know what town, though."

"How long will you have her?"

"I don't know." Mrs. Anderson became sort of sad. "Her mother's a crack addict. She's so caught up with getting the drugs she needs that I think she literally forgets she has a baby to care for. That's why she left Melody alone for two days. And that wasn't the first time."

I looked at the baby. Her hair was behaving better today because she'd just had a bath. It fell in little curls that bounced when she wiggled. I thought it was nice for her to be with Mrs. Anderson before she was big enough to realize that her mom had forgotten about her. It would save her a lot of hurt.

"What's her last name?" I asked.

"It's Elliot. Melody Elliot."

I nodded. "Sounds good."

"Almost as good as Charlette Fowler," said Mrs. Anderson.

"Charlie," I corrected. "Charlie Fowler."

"You're going into sixth grade, aren't you?" Mrs. Anderson asked.

I nodded. "I'm sort of surprised I am because my grades aren't very good. I thought they might actually flunk me this year."

"Truancy, right?" said Mrs. Anderson.

I was surprised that she knew about that. What else did she know?

"Well, no more." She smiled warmly and reached over the seat to pat my knee. "You're one smart cookie, Charlie. When you go to school every day like you're supposed to, you'll find yourself doing very well."

Not only did this lady need glasses; she needed to start telling the truth.

Melody chose that instant to grab a handful of my hair and ram it into her mouth.

"Yo, kid! That hurts!"

I squeezed her little hand to make her let go. Instead, she screamed and grabbed another handful, then began to cry with great enthusiasm.

"I didn't mean to hurt her!" I said defensively, my head bent at an odd angle as Melody tugged and wailed. "She's the one inflicting pain!"

"Of course you didn't mean to hurt her," Mrs. Anderson agreed. "You'll have better luck if you pry her fingers loose one at a time." And she turned around and began talking to Mr. Anderson.

While I slowly undid Melody's fingers, I stared at the back of Mrs. Anderson's head. This lady certainly didn't do things the way my mom did.

First off, Mom said I could stay home from school any day I wanted to. Everyone knew school was a waste of time. And if she'd been here when Melody started crying, she'd have let me know how stupid I was, picking on a poor baby, for Pete's sake, and making her cry.

It was going to be hard getting used to someone else's way of doing things. But I hoped I wouldn't be with the Andersons that long. Mom was probably trying to get me back already.

I got my hair free of Melody's clutches by the time we pulled up in front of the church.

Mom always made fun of churches, saying all the people who went were idiots for letting those phony ministers take their money. She liked to watch the TV preachers and mock them, even when she was sober.

I climbed out of the car and stood there trying to be invisible. Adults in dresses and suits hurried all around me, waving to each other and talking, talking, talking. Little kids were being dragged along by their hands, and some of them were not happy. One little boy kept saying, "No, Mommy, no, Mommy, no, Mommy," but his mother didn't pay any attention.

Suddenly I saw a familiar figure.

"Shannon!" I yelled before I thought.

Shannon and everyone else within earshot turned. I made believe I didn't see anyone but her, and I made believe I wasn't embarrassed.

"Charlie!"

Shannon Symmonds had been in my cabin at Harmony Hill, and she had helped me have a not-too-bad time at camp. Now she took me with her and led me to the room where our Sunday school class met.

"Hi, Charlie." It was Gail, who had been the nurse at Camp Harmony Hill. "It's good to see you again."

"Gail's our teacher," Shannon whispered as we took our seats in a room filled with lots of talking, giggling girls.

I didn't say much; I just watched. I recognized Shannon's friends who had been at Harmony Hill too, but in a different cabin. They were Dee, Cammi, Alysha, and Bethany. They seemed nice enough. But the girl who really caught my eye was someone named Brooke. What a priss! She obviously thought she was someone very special, and she seemed to expect everyone else to think so too. I decided then and there not to like her.

I guess Gail was a good Sunday school teacher. I

didn't have anything to compare her with, but I didn't fall asleep. Most of the stuff she said I didn't understand, but she did say one thing I'd heard before at camp: God loves us very much.

"He loves us so much that He made each of us special," Gail said. "He loves us so much, the Bible says, that He even knows the number of hairs on our heads."

Shannon and the other girls seemed to agree. They nodded their heads as she talked.

I wasn't so sure I wanted God to love me. He'd just want me to love Him back. My experience with love was that it hurt too much. After all, if I didn't love Mom so much, I wouldn't care that she liked drinking more than me.

God, I thought, I hope *You won't get mad, but I don't think I want any more love in my life.*

Sitting at the Andersons' dining room table, I understood why they skipped lunch on Sunday. They ate dinner in the middle of the day!

Apparently I was the only one who thought this arrangement was strange. Shannon and her mom and Dee and all her family were guests, and they all acted as if this were normal. I figured church people must always eat dinner in the afternoon on Sundays.

I felt a little uneasy eating with all these strangers, especially Dee's father. He was the minister at the Andersons' church. He seemed like a nice-enough man, but after all Mom's comments about how phony and money-hungry ministers were, I wasn't certain what to expect. I wouldn't have been surprised if he'd passed an offering plate between dinner and dessert.

But he didn't, and neither did anyone else. They were all pleasant and very kind to me, except for Dee's eight-year-old twin brothers. They were obnoxious, as boys always are.

After dinner Mrs. Anderson asked us girls to put Melody to bed while she and the other ladies cleaned up.

Poor Melody was falling asleep in her high chair. Her little head kept bobbing up and down like those little dolls people put in the back window of their cars. I carried her upstairs with Shannon and Dee trailing behind.

"Let me rock her," begged Shannon as she sat in the rocking chair in Melody's room.

"And I'll read her a story," said Dee.

Melody woke up just long enough to make the girls happy, smiling and gurgling at them.

When Dee finished her story, I took the baby. She rested her head on my shoulder and promptly went to sleep. Just *boom*, she was gone.

"What do I do now?" I whispered. "Do I have to hold her until she wakes up?"

What a terrible thought.

"Just put her down," Dee said. "She'll keep right on sleeping."

"On her tummy," Shannon said.

"On her tummy?"

Shannon and Dee both nodded as though they knew they were right.

I shrugged. I bent over the crib and put Melody on her tummy. She snuffled and squirmed a little, but she stayed asleep. The three of us stood by the crib and stared at her.

"She's so cute!" Shannon said. "I love her curls. I wish I had a baby sister."

"No, you don't," said Dee. "It would just grow up to be eight years old like the twins."

"My mom says that babies just mess up your life," I said.

Though I'm not certain she's the best judge of things like this, I thought, but out of loyalty I didn't say it out loud.

"Let's go for a walk," said Dee. "We can show Charlie a little bit of East Edge."

"Sure," said Shannon, "but don't try to tell me you're doing this for Charlie. You just can't stand to be still."

Dee didn't deny the charge. Instead she said, "At least I don't bob all over the place like Alysha. She sat behind me in church a couple of weeks ago and kept kicking my pew. I thought my teeth would fall out before Dad stopped talking!"

We ambled slowly down Olive Street. It was a nice neighborhood, not rich, but certainly not poor. The houses all looked comfortable and welcoming. People had planted nice bushes and flowers, and they kept their lawns mowed.

I thought of the little apartment in downtown West Chester that Mom and I lived in—and would live in again if Mom remembered to pay the rent until I got home. One bedroom, a leaky bathroom, and a living room full of junky furniture. The kitchen was tiny, and if I looked in the refrigerator, I always found more booze than food. I made a mental note to check Mrs. Anderson's fridge when I had a chance.

We turned down Thirteenth Avenue, heading toward Lincoln Highway. Shannon and Dee talked about people I'd never met, but I didn't mind. I just listened with half an ear and wondered where Mom was. Was she doing all right without me to watch over her? When she was drinking, her gorgeous blue eyes clouded, and she couldn't make choices. I had to make them for her.

"Mom," I'd said more than once, "why do you drink so much? How can you stand not being in control of yourself? Why are you willing to let your kid make your decisions?"

She'd laugh and shake her finger at me. "You

think I don't know what's going on? Of course I do." And she'd flop in the best living room chair and fall asleep, snoring gently.

I sighed as we turned the corner onto Lincoln Highway. Big old houses lined the street except for one apartment building. Most of the houses were doubles, sort of like townhouses but not in a big row. Most of them needed paint.

"See that house, Charlie?" Shannon pointed across the street. "Those guys are always the first in town with their Christmas decorations. My mom says that soon they'll be putting them up the day after Halloween."

But I wasn't really listening. I was staring at the apartment building. I couldn't believe my eyes!

"I'll be right back," I mumbled and raced down the sidewalk.

A woman was walking up to a car parked at the curb. She had pretty blond hair pulled back with a barrette at her neck, but some curls had escaped around her face. Her eyes were protected by large mirror sunglasses, and she was wearing a light-blue blouse, jeans, and four-inch spike heels. She sort of teetered when she walked. I hoped she wasn't drunk because she was certain to lose her balance in those things if she was.

She heard my pounding footsteps and turned to see what was going on.

"Mom!" I skidded to a stop beside her.

I reached out to hug her, but she stepped back, her arms up to hold me off.

"Don't want to mess up my hair," she said, but she smiled so I wouldn't be hurt. "It took too long to get it fixed."

"Oh, Mom, I've missed you!"

I could see my reflection in her sunglasses. I looked lost and upset.

"What are you doing in East Edge?" I asked. "Are you looking for me?"

Mom peered at me. "You're being taken care of, aren't you? I called Mrs. Pengalli last week, and she said Children's Services had you."

Mrs. Pengalli was our neighbor in the apartment next to ours, and she crammed it with five kids and a lazy husband who never worked because of a "back condition."

"Back condition, schmack condition," Mom always said. "He hasn't got a back condition when it comes to bending over a pool table all night."

But Mrs. Pengalli was nice. "I don't like to see kids treated bad," she told me frequently. "Is your mama being good to you?"

The worse Mom was, the more loudly I told Mrs. Pengalli everything was all right. I knew she would report us if I ever gave her a reason.

"Yeah, Children's Services has me," I said.

Mom nodded. "I bet it was Mrs. Pengalli who called the cops."

I'd already figured that out.

"She wasn't very nice to me on the phone." Mom looked hurt at the memory. "She called me a lousy mother."

"Don't pay any attention to her, Mom. I think you're fine, and that's what counts, right?"

Mom's face cleared. "You're a good girl, Charlie. Where are you living?"

"I'm living with a family just around the corner." I pointed vaguely in the direction of the Andersons' house. "But I can't wait to be back with you!"

"Why? Aren't they nice?"

"They're very nice," I said. "But you're my mother. When are you going to get me back? Have you got a lawyer yet? You'll probably need to go to court."

"I'm not going to court, Charlie," she said happily. "We're going to California!"

"You're kidding!" I caught her excitement, and her sunglasses reflected my happy face. "California! When are we leaving? How are we going? How can we afford it?"

She took her sunglasses off, and I saw how bloodshot her eyes were. She shook her head. "We're not going, Charlie, you and me. *We're* going, Dink and me." She pointed to the car.

For the first time I realized that a man was sitting in the driver's seat listening to our conversation.

"Dink, honey, this is Charlie. You remember I told you about her?"

He looked at me blankly. "I thought Charlie was a boy."

"You were wrong, Dink," Mom said, leaning down and kissing him on the forehead. There was a lot of forehead to kiss because he was real bald. He made up for the lack of hair on his head with a frizzy red beard sprouting from his face.

Ugly man, I thought. Ugly, hateful man!

"Come on, Flo," he said. "Get your cute little self in here so we can get going." He turned the key, and the engine sprang to life. Mom giggled and hurried around to the passenger side, patting me on the hand as she passed.

She didn't even look back as they drove off.

I stood staring down the road long after Mom's car had disappeared. My mouth was probably hanging open in disbelief.

"Close your mouth, Charlie," Mom always said. "Something's going to fly in some day and choke you."

"Who was that?" Shannon asked.

I jumped. I hadn't realized she and Dee had caught up with me.

I just shook my head. It wasn't much of an answer, but I was afraid that if I opened my mouth at all, I would start to cry. Buckets. I'd spout more water than Niagara Falls.

I couldn't believe it! Mom was going to California with some bald guy named Dink—what kind of a dumb name was Dink?—and she was leaving me behind! And she was happy.

I felt like I had a knife in my heart, like one of those pictures of a heart with little drops of blood dripping out. I felt like I was dying.

Where had this Dink person come from? I'd never heard of him, so she must have just met him. She was going to California with some bearded stranger, and she was leaving me behind.

She's leaving me behind. I'll never see her again, and she doesn't even care! She's leaving me behind! I couldn't get those words out of my head.

"Never get involved with babies, Charlie," she always said. "They mess up your life."

I'd always thought she meant babies in general, little weepy, sniveling kids, the ones you see crabbing in the grocery store. But she hadn't. She'd meant me!

I turned and started walking. I stared at the sidewalk so I wouldn't have to talk to Shannon and Dee who walked with me, one on each side. I knew they were looking at each other in confusion, trying to figure out what was wrong.

"Who was she, Charlie?" Shannon asked. "What did she say to upset you so much?"

Since I couldn't trust myself to answer, I ignored the question, concentrating instead on putting one foot in front of the other. I just wanted to get to the Andersons' without my rubber knees giving out and depositing me on the pavement. I wanted to get to the house without throwing up Mrs. Anderson's Sunday dinner on some stranger's lawn.

The Dennings and Mrs. Symmonds were standing outside, talking to the Andersons and waiting for us to come back so they could leave. I kept my head down, ignoring everybody, and walked into the house and up to my room without saying a word to anyone. I was a zombie. When I glanced in the mirror, I half expected to see my eyes glowing like in an old movie.

Instead I saw the saddest face I'd ever seen.

I flopped on my rosebud quilt and stared at the ceiling. Now that I could cry without making a fool of myself, no tears would come.

I curled up in a little ball and tried to forget Mom's happy smile. *She's leaving me behind!* I punched my pillow a few times and wondered what I'd ever done to deserve such a terrible thing happening to me.

God, is this how You show people you love them? By letting their moms run away? God, she's leaving me behind! She's leaving me behind!

I know it sounds impossible, but I must have fallen asleep, because two hours had passed when Mrs. Anderson's voice floated up the stairs.

"Charlie, come on down. I've made you a grilled cheese sandwich."

When I walked into the kitchen, all I could think of was old "Leave It to Beaver" and "Father Knows Best" reruns. Everything was so cute and cheery, from the flowered curtains to the potato chips on the table in a basket, for Pete's sake. What was wrong with the bag they came in? Mrs. Anderson was feeding Melody, who was slobbering happily in her high chair. Mr. Anderson was reading about the Philadelphia Eagles in the newspaper. Everyone was smiling and happy. I thought I'd puke.

I flopped into my chair and stared at my sandwich. I knew I'd get sick if I ate it, but who cared? I grabbed a half and took a bite, then another.

"Did you and the girls have a nice walk this afternoon?" Mrs. Anderson asked.

"Swell," I said. "Just great." I gave her a huge phony smile.

"What's wrong, Charlie?"

Mrs. Anderson showed more concern for me in that instant than Mom had shown in my whole life. I'd never felt so angry as I did at that moment. Why should this stranger care more about me than my own mother? It wasn't fair!

"Leave me alone!" I yelled. "Just leave me alone!"

Mrs. Anderson didn't act the least bit shocked or mad. If anything, her concern deepened.

"Shannon and Dee said you spoke with some woman, and she upset you."

I snorted. Upset was much too mild a word for what I felt.

"Who was she, honey?"

Honey, schmoney. I stared at my grilled cheese.

"Was it your mother?"

I jumped as though a bee had stung me, and I threw my sandwich across the table. "Leave me alone!" I yelled again. "Just leave me alone!"

My loud voice scared Melody, and she began to cry. That made me feel guilty, so I got mad at her, too.

"Shut up, you little whiner," I said. "Stuff your stupid food in your mouth and shut up."

In answer, Melody reached her little hands out toward me, tears still sitting in her eyes.

"She wants you, Charlie," said Mrs. Anderson. "Here. You feed her dessert." She handed me a jar of strained peaches and a spoon.

I was so surprised that I forgot to be mad.

"Just take a spoonful and put it in her mouth," Mrs. Anderson said. She turned her back on me and began tidying up her already tidy kitchen counter.

I stared at Melody, and she stared at me. She had almost as much food on her bib as I held in the jar of peaches. This was not a neat child.

I held a spoonful of peaches in front of her mouth. "Open up, kid."

And miracle of miracles, she did. In no time she had eaten all the peaches and was gurgling happily at me.

Mrs. Anderson handed me a wet cloth. "Wipe her mouth and hands off. Then take her into the living room and play with her while Mr. Anderson and I finish cleaning up out here."

Melody and I played on the living room floor until she had to go to bed. By "play" I mean I let her pull my hair and gnaw on it while I tried not to think about Mom. After Melody left, I turned on the TV.

I've always used TV to escape from my problems. I can watch it by the hour, and it doesn't matter whether I like what's on or not. I'm just glad for the noise and the company and the distraction.

"Just so you know, Charlie," Mr. Anderson said, now studying the business section of the newspaper, "the TV goes off at eleven tonight."

I looked at him in disbelief. "That early?" I thought he must be joking.

But at eleven o'clock he said, "Time." He aimed the remote control at the set, and the picture disappeared.

I sat up and looked at him. "Hey, I was watching that!"

"It's time for bed," he said. He smiled. "On weeknights I usually turn it off at ten."

Ten! Was the guy serious? I usually watched until well after midnight. Sometimes I fell asleep on the sofa watching.

"Just because you want it off doesn't mean I do." My voice had a sharp edge to it. What right did he have to tell me I couldn't watch TV?

"Charlie, we have certain patterns around here, and while you're our guest, you'll follow them with us." Mr. Anderson didn't raise his voice, but he was like a rock. He wasn't going to be moved.

That didn't mean I wasn't going to try. I wasn't at all sleepy, thanks to my nap, and I wanted to watch TV.

"You can go to bed if you want to," I said, trying hard to sound reasonable. "I'll just turn the sound down."

He shook his head. "You're only eleven, Charlie. You need a good night's sleep."

"Tomorrow's Labor Day. I'll sleep in."

"I don't mind if you sleep in," he said. "I hope to do so myself if Melody'll let me. But we'll all go to bed at the same time."

"That's not fair!" After the rough day I'd had, I wasn't about to be pushed around. Mom always said I was nice enough unless I lost my temper, and then I was terrible. And it was true. I was proud of how terrible I could be.

Mrs. Anderson came into the room. "Bed will sure feel good tonight! I love having guests for dinner, but it always wear me out."

I turned my anger to her. "He says I have to turn the TV off! Tell him it's okay if I stay up!"

Mrs. Anderson shook her head. "House policy."

"But it's not fair!"

"It probably won't make you any happier," Mrs. Anderson said, "but we had the same rules when our kids were still at home."

"You can make any rule you want to for your kids, but I'm not any old kid that you can boss around," I snapped. "Nobody tells me what to do. If I want to stay up late, I stay up late."

Mr. Anderson nodded. "Perhaps in the past you did, but here we go to bed at a normal hour."

"Normal! Who are you trying to kid? No one goes to bed this early!"

Mr. Anderson got to his feet and headed out of the room. "Last one out, don't forget to turn the lights off." He paused in the doorway and looked at me. "I expect you to be in your room in five minutes."

I blew up. "Who do you think you are, telling me what to do? Just because Children's Services dumped me here doesn't mean you're my boss! I'll go to bed when I want to, and I'll watch TV when I want to! I didn't ask to come here! And I won't listen to your stupid rules!"

"Five minutes, Charlie," he answered.

I spun around and grabbed the remote control. I'd show him! If he thought he could order me around like some little kid, he was mistaken!

The TV blinked on and the sound poured out. It was a news program, so I began flicking through the channels.

Mrs. Anderson walked over to me, took the control right out of my hand, and turned the set off.

"Three minutes, Charlie." She set the remote on the TV and left the room.

I tried to remember the last time anyone had told me what to do. I couldn't think of a time, unless you wanted to count teachers. And I usually didn't listen to them.

Suddenly I had an idea. I thumped my way upstairs to my room, slamming the door so they would know what I thought of them and their stupid rules.

I heard Melody cry out in her sleep at the loud noise, but I was so angry I didn't care.

I lay on top of my quilt and stared angrily at the ceiling. Deserted by my mother and ordered around by some people I never asked to live with! What a day! Well, I'd show them! I'd show them all that Charlie Fowler couldn't be beaten!

I waited until I heard no more noise or movement in the house. Then I made myself wait ten more minutes. When I thought it was safe, I got up, tiptoed to the door, opened it carefully and listened. Silence.

Feeling smug, I tiptoed downstairs to the living room. I moved as quietly as possible, just the way I did on mornings Mom had a hangover. I turned on the TV and settled onto the sofa to watch. It was a little chilly, and I wished I had thought to bring my quilt with me. I was afraid to risk going back for it. I huddled in the sofa corner, stacking the throw pillows around me for warmth.

There wasn't much to watch except old movies. I watched John Wayne win the West and was really enjoying Charles Bronson doing his usual blood-and-guts thing when I fell asleep.

I woke up at first light, trying to figure out where I was.

When I remembered, I panicked. I had to turn the TV off and get to bed before the Andersons woke up and found me.

It was then I realized that the TV was already off, and I was covered by a blanket.

It was five o'clock Labor Day afternoon when we drove between the stone lions at the entrance of Hibernia Park. We were going to have a picnic. Let's just hear that drum roll and shoot off those fireworks.

It's not that I really minded having a picnic. I hardly ever get to go on one, so I enjoy them when I can. It's just that my life had become so weird that nothing sounded fun.

I'd slept as late as I could after sneaking back into bed. I didn't want a lecture on obedience and how I should appreciate all the Andersons were doing for me.

When I finally got up about noon, no one even mentioned my TV caper. They just fed me lunch and asked me to clean my room.

"That's child labor; the cops will get you," I said, only half kidding.

Mrs. Anderson smiled. "Your suitcase still has some of your camp clothes in it, and it looks as though you're using your floor for a hamper. Just pick things up, put them where they belong, and make your bed. We'll leave for our picnic as soon as Melody wakes up from her nap."

I stood in my doorway and studied my room. My half-packed suitcase lay on the floor in front of the window. My clothes for the last two days lay wherever I'd been standing when I took them off. And my bed looked like a giant electric beater had been stirring up the sheets. I walked over to the bed and flopped down on my back. I lay staring at nothing, seeing Mom's happy face and hearing her giggle as she climbed into dumb Dink's car.

So she'd never been the world's greatest mom. If I were honest, I'd have to admit she'd never even been very good. But she was mine, and I didn't want to lose her. I wanted her back.

The tears came and overflowed my eyes, rolling back into my hair. My nose stopped up so badly I couldn't breathe, and my head throbbed. I cried, sniffed, and coughed, trying not to make enough noise for anyone to hear. The last thing I wanted was pity.

Rotten life, I thought. Rotten, rotten, rotten life.

When I heard Melody cooing down the hall, I was surprised. She certainly hadn't slept long. I looked at the clock radio.

4:30! I'd always been good at putting my mind in neutral because things hurt less that way—but two hours of ceiling-staring was ridiculous!

I leaped up when I heard Mrs. Anderson coming up the stairs. I grabbed my quilt and threw it over the crumpled sheets. It looked a bit lumpy, but maybe Mrs. Anderson wouldn't notice. I grabbed a handful of dirty clothes and stuffed them in the hamper in the closet just as Mrs. Anderson stopped in my doorway.

"Almost done," I said, grabbing another handful of dirty clothes.

She was studying my bed. "Very interesting set of mountains and valleys you've got there, Charlie. Did you have to work hard to achieve that effect?"

"Uh," I said.

"That's what I thought," she said. "We'll be leaving in about ten minutes."

Hibernia Park was nicer than I expected. It was really big, not like the little parks in West Chester.

There was a fishing pond for little kids, a big mansion that you could tour, lots of fields for baseball and volleyball, a stream for walking along or fishing in, a camping area for tents or trailers, pavilions you could rent for big group picnics, and trees—lots and lots of trees.

We staked our claim to a table in the grove of trees near the parking area. While Mr. Anderson lit a fire in the grate and had a great time playing chef, Mrs. Anderson put a tablecloth on our table and got out the food. Somehow I didn't think she had bought the potato salad and coleslaw already made at the grocery store.

I watched Mr. Anderson flipping the hamburgers.

"Have you ever thought of getting him a big white hat like they wear in restaurants?" I asked.

"Not a bad idea," Mrs. Anderson said. "I'll pass it on to one of our kids for next Father's Day."

After we finished eating, I took Melody for a ride on the swings. She sat on my lap as I slowly pushed us back and forth. I couldn't do anything very wild because I had to hold her with one arm and the swing with the other. But Melody was happy. She didn't know swings could go right up to the sky, especially ones with long chains like these.

When I got tired of the swings, we sat in the sandbox for a while. At first Melody didn't like the sand. I guess it was the first time she'd ever seen it, and it felt funny to her. I drizzled some onto her foot, and she just sat and stared for a minute. Then she pulled her foot back and turned a horrified face to me.

"It's okay, baby," I said. "Look." I drizzled some sand onto my foot.

She wasn't convinced.

I patted the sand with my hand. "Come on, Melody. Pat the sand."

She stared at me for a long time, but finally she laid her hand on the sand.

"Good girl," I said and drizzled sand on her hand.

This time she didn't get upset. She dug her little fingers into the sand, got a fistful, and tried to eat it before I realized what she was going to do.

I pulled her hand out of her mouth. "Yo, Melody. Sand is for playing, not eating."

She grinned at me with a little sand-and-slobber beard on her chin.

"Look," I said, and I drew a flower in the sand. I drew her lots of things—a clown, a sailboat, a house, a baby.

"That's you," I said. "See the curls?"

She gurgled, telling me how lovely the portrait was.

"Come on, Charlie," Mr. Anderson called, gesturing to Melody and me with his arm. "We're going to take a walk down by the creek."

A walk by the creek. Somehow I wasn't excited. But as I said, nothing could excite me just then.

I hugged Melody to me and followed the Andersons without enthusiasm. The baby grabbed a handful of my hair and began chomping happily.

"If anything can get me to cut my hair, kid," I told Melody, "it's you. Someone ought to teach you that hair isn't for eating. It's for keeping your head warm in winter."

Melody took my hair out of her mouth long enough to explain why she liked to chew on it. At least I guess that's what she told me. Who knows?

When she laid her head on my shoulder and reached out a hand to pull on my nose, a fierce concern for her swept over me, surprising me. I felt like a mama bird protecting her babies, all ready to squawk and dive-bomb anyone who looked threatening.

"Look, Melody," I said, "life can be like a punch in the stomach sometimes. I'd protect you if I could. I sure don't want you to watch your mother drive away from you, especially with someone like dumb Dink. Stay with the Andersons, okay? They could be like your grandmom and grandpop."

We walked down a path until we came to a stream gurgling over rocks in little, very little, waterfalls. It was a pretty stream, the kind you could sit beside for a long time. We all sat on a couple of big rocks and just watched the water flow by. After a few minutes I took my shoes off and put my feet in the water. I was surprised at how cold it felt.

"Is it too cold to put the baby's feet in?" I asked.

Mrs. Anderson shook her head. "She'd probably like it. She likes her bath."

Melody loved it, kicking her feet and reaching out to touch the water. Mrs. Anderson took her from me and held her so she could slap the water. She giggled and wiggled until she made a big splash that got her in the face. Talk about startled!

I stood up and began wading in the water. It was fun to take step after step and see how deep the stream was. Most of the time the water only came to my ankles, but there were a couple of deeper spots. When I found a place where the water was above my knees but below my shorts, I decided that was deep enough.

I walked back to the rock where the Andersons and Melody were sitting and watched Mr. Anderson skip pebbles across the water. No matter how hard I tried, I couldn't do it. My pebbles just sank.

"Come here, Melody," I said, tired of failing. "Come walk in the water with Charlie."

I reached out, and Mrs. Anderson passed the baby to me. I took her under the arms, facing her away from me, and lowered her until her feet touched the water. Immediately she began to kick and squeal with joy.

I took a couple of steps with her, laughing at her laughter. I hadn't expected to laugh ever again, at least not for a long, long time, but Melody was so funny. She certainly made life at the Andersons bearable. Not exactly good, you know, but not bad either.

A clump of leaves floating on the surface of the water swirled our way.

"Look, Melody," I said. "Pretty leaves."

I hitched her up under one arm and reached to catch the leaves as they floated past. I missed, so I tried again, stretching as far as I could. As I did so, I stepped on a mossy, slippery rock and lost my balance. I tried to stay upright, but when my foot slipped, I stumbled into a hole and went down with a splash. I opened my mouth to scream just as the water closed over my head.

Melody went flying right out of my arms and into the creek.

I came up out of the water sputtering and spitting and gagging, then promptly lost my footing as I stepped in the hole again and went down and under a second time.

In my mind I was screaming, "Melody! Melody!" In reality I was swallowing water so fast I couldn't say a thing. As I struggled to my feet again, I was choking and crying and retching. I staggered around like a fish flopping on dry land. I pulled at my hair, trying to get it out of my eyes.

I was scared to death that I had killed the baby.

Suddenly a hand grabbed one of my flailing arms and a strong arm went around my waist.

"Easy, Charlie. It's all right." Mr. Anderson was standing in the water with me, keeping me from falling again. His pants were wet and his shoes would never be the same. "Just bend over and cough as much as you can," he instructed.

I looked at him wildly. "Where's the baby?" I tried to say. All that came out was an inelegant gagging, burping noise.

"Melody's fine," he said. "Listen."

Her cries were the sweetest, most wonderful sound I had ever heard. I finally got my hair out of my face enough to see her safe in Mrs. Anderson's arms, soaking wet, red in the face, bawling like an angry cat, but obviously unharmed.

Thank You, God!

We splashed clumsily to Melody and Mrs. Anderson, who were standing on our large rock at the edge of the stream.

"Is she okay?" I asked in a whisper. At least I wasn't retching anymore.

"She's fine," Mrs. Anderson said. "Wet and scared and a little angry, but fine."

I studied Melody from head to toe, afraid I'd find something wrong in spite of the Andersons' assurances. When I was sure she was truly all right, I sank down on the rock and started to cry.

"I'm sorry," I mumbled through my tears. "I'm sorry, I'm sorry, I'm sorry."

Mrs. Anderson handed Melody to Mr. Anderson,

who was quietly dripping on our rock. She sat down beside me, put her arm around my shoulders, and pulled me to her. She was soft and cushiony and comforting, and I couldn't stop crying.

"I almost killed her," I whispered through my tears. "I almost killed her."

Mrs. Anderson kissed the top of my head. I don't think anyone had ever kissed the top of my head before.

"No, you didn't, Charlie," she said. "All you did was fall. Melody almost landed in my arms—all I had to do was reach out and grab her. You were the one we were worried about. You were the one who went down and under. You were the one who was choking and gagging. You were the one who cut herself."

"I cut myself?" I squinted through my tears and saw my left shin and knee gushing blood. "I never felt a thing."

"Well, we're just glad you're not really hurt." She gave my shoulders a squeeze. "Don, give me your handkerchief."

Mr. Anderson handed over a wet white square which Mrs. Anderson placed over my shin. "Hold this, Charlie," she said. "Press it against your leg as hard as you can."

"Is this how you took care of your kids when they hurt themselves?" I asked, doing as she said with the handkerchief. "Is this what real mothers do?"

As soon as the words were out of my mouth, I realized what dumb questions they were. I usually don't say things that dumb. It must have been from my dunking. Water on the brain.

I saw Mrs. Anderson exchange a look with Mr. Anderson, but she didn't answer. I think she knew that no matter what she said, it would make my mother look bad.

Suddenly I felt very tired and lost and alone. I rested my head on Mrs. Anderson's shoulder.

"That lady I saw yesterday," I said. "You know, the one Shannon and Dee told you about? It was Mom."

Mrs. Anderson nodded. "I thought it might have been. What happened that upset you so?"

I started to cry again. I'd probably cried more in the last two days than in the whole rest of my life put together.

"She—" Sob, sob, sob. I took a deep breath and tried again. "She's going to California."

The Andersons exchanged another look, but I didn't care.

"She told you this?" Mrs. Anderson asked.

I nodded. "She was going with some bald guy named Dink, and she was all excited and happy." I lifted the handkerchief off my shin, which wasn't bleeding at the moment, and moved it to my knee, which was. "She was very happy."

"Oh, Charlie," Mrs. Anderson said, resting her cheek on the top of my head. "I'm so sorry."

And she cried with me for a few minutes. I couldn't believe it! No one had ever cried with me before. At first I felt awkward as we snuffled together, but I decided I liked the cozy, well-somebody-cares feeling her tears gave me.

We walked back to our picnic table in silence, Mr. Anderson squishing with every step. He and Melody and I left a clear trail behind us as we dripped up the path. Mrs. Anderson insisted that I carry Melody.

At first I protested. "But I'm wet."

"So's she," said Mrs. Anderson as she pressed the baby into my arms. "Take her."

I was afraid to hold her at first. What if I turned out to be as clumsy on dry land as I'd been in the water?

"It's like falling off a horse," Mrs. Anderson said.

I looked at her in confusion. What did a horse

have to do with anything?

"When you fall off a horse," she said, "they tell you to get right back on. Otherwise you might become so afraid you'll fall another time that you'll never ride again."

"I get it," I said. "I'm the guy who fell off, right?"

Mrs. Anderson put Melody in my arms, and in no time I was comfortable carrying the squirmy bundle. In fact I was sorry when I had to put her in her car seat for the ride home. Worn out by her adventure, she fell asleep before we were even out of the park.

Mr. Anderson carried all the picnic stuff to the kitchen while Mrs. Anderson put Melody to bed. Somehow there seemed to be a lot more stuff to unload than there had been to pack when we left.

I was sitting at the kitchen table finishing off the potato chips when Mrs. Anderson played back the telephone answering machine.

"Ann, this is Dr. Linton. I must see you and Melody—and Don if possible—first thing tomorrow morning. I'll be at the office by nine."

Dr. Linton's office looked like most doctors' offices I'd been in except that everything was planned for kids. There were a few adult-sized chairs, but there were lots of little chairs, a little table, blocks, books, Matchbox cars, and a TV playing *The Little Mermaid.*

Mrs. Anderson had brought me along because she wanted Dr. Linton to look at my knee and shin. "I think you may need stitches," she said.

Just what I need, I thought. More pain.

Mr. Anderson hadn't been able to come with us because he had to fly to Boston for some kind of business. He wouldn't be back until Wednesday night.

Because we had such an early appointment, there weren't many people in the waiting room.

There was a baby with a very runny nose who sort of sputtered when he breathed. He sat on his mother's lap and napped. His mother didn't look much older than me. Another girl was with them, and she kept whispering to the young mother and looking at us. Mrs. Anderson didn't seem to notice, but they made me feel strange.

When the nurse called us, we were taken to a little room in the back.

"The doctor will be with you in a few minutes," the nurse said, leaving us.

"Is it against the doctors' code to see patients right away?" I asked no one in particular. "They all make you wait."

Mrs. Anderson smiled. "Usually the nurse weighs and measures the baby and things like that, so a few minutes is good. But I know what you mean."

When Dr. Linton finally did come, I almost laughed. He looked just like Bill Cosby.

He saw my face and nodded. "Terrible, isn't it? All the kids call me Dr. Huxtable. Do you want to take those Band-aids off, or shall I?"

I hate it when you have to rip Band-aids off. They take all your hair and skin with them. I took a deep breath and pulled. My leg looked like it belonged to a Chihuahua Hairless.

Dr. Linton studied my wounds for a minute. They really were gaping and ugly.

"How'd you do this?" he asked.

"I fell in the stream and cut myself on something."

"You don't know what?"

I shook my head.

He glanced at Mrs. Anderson.

She shook her head, too.

"Huh," Dr. Linton said. Then he got up and opened the door. "Martie," he called, "tetanus shot."

"A shot?" I said. "Do I really need one?"

"When did you last have one?" he asked.

"Who knows?" I said.

"You need one. You don't need stitches though. Keep these covered until there are good scabs. Change the bandage every time it gets wet. And don't get the wounds dirty."

I've always hated shots. I know they're necessary to make you well or keep you well, but I still hate them. I don't even think they hurt all that much. I just hate the idea of someone sticking something in me on purpose.

"If you feel like this about shots," Mom said

the last time I was really sick, "I'll never have to worry about you shooting up drugs."

The very thought of giving myself a shot makes me shudder.

The door opened, and the nurse came in armed with a needle at least fifteen feet long.

"Ann," Dr. Linton said to Mrs. Anderson, "why don't you and Melody come with me to my office while Martie gives Charlie her shot? Kay Mallin is there, too."

Mrs. Anderson took a deep breath, gathered Melody up, and followed the doctor.

"Is that Mrs. Mallin, the social worker?" I asked the nurse.

"I think so," she said, flicking her finger against the part of the needle that held the medicine. Getting out all the bubbles so she wouldn't kill me by injecting me with air.

If it was supposed to make me feel better about the shot, it didn't work. I decided I'd wonder why Mrs. Mallin was there; then I wouldn't be able to think about the shot because I can't think of two things at the same time.

Mrs. Mallin was the caseworker who had delivered me to the Andersons. Why would she be meeting with Mrs. Anderson and Dr. Linton? Was there something wrong with me? Or about me?

"This won't be too bad," said Martie, her thumb on the needle plunger. "Hold your sleeve up, please."

I lifted my shirt sleeve, turned my head away, and scrunched up my face, anticipating the pain. All I felt were a sharp prick and a little pressure as she pushed the medicine in.

I looked at Martie in amazement. "You're good."

She smiled. "I get lots of practice. You should try giving a shot to a two year old who doesn't want it. That's real warfare. Why don't you sit in the waiting room until Mrs. Anderson's finished?"

I was glad for the suggestion. I sat in one of the little chairs near the TV and watched *The Little Mermaid*. The young mom and her snotty baby weren't there anymore, but the friend who kept staring at us was. So were two newborn babies and their mothers.

I lost track of how long I waited for Mrs. Anderson, but it had to be a long time because I got to see most of the movie. The young mom and her baby came out, the kid blowing bubbles with his nose. It was gross.

"Come on, Cheryl," the mom said to her friend. She didn't even glance at me.

Cheryl followed, then stopped at the door and gave me a long, hard look. I hate to be stared at. It's so impolite. I stared back.

When Mrs. Anderson finally came out, she looked like she'd been crying. She didn't stop at the desk to pay or anything; she just walked straight out the door. I think she'd forgotten I was there.

I jumped out of my seat and followed her. I climbed into the front passenger side as she buckled Melody into her car seat.

She bent over and kissed Melody very gently and ran her hand over the little girl's head. Then she stood up with a loud sniff, walked around the car, and got in behind the wheel. She sort of jumped when she saw me.

"Charlie!" She smiled at me sadly. "I'm sorry."

I knew she meant for forgetting me.

"Was your shot too terrible?" she asked, trying to be interested.

I shook my head. "That nurse is pretty good. I hardly felt a thing."

But already she wasn't hearing what I said. She just sat behind the wheel without moving, lost in her thoughts.

I turned around and looked at Melody. Was

something wrong with her? She grinned at me and reached for my hair, but I was too far away. She certainly looked fine to me. I looked back at Mrs. Anderson. What was going on?

Finally she started the car. She pulled out into traffic and drove slowly home. She didn't say a word.

Melody was jabbering happily. I turned around to smile at her when I noticed that in the car behind us were the young mother and her whispery friend Cheryl from the doctor's office. The mom must be older than she looked to be driving.

They were still behind us when we pulled into the Andersons' drive. I waved to them as they drove slowly by.

I slid out of my seat and began undoing Melody's belts and buckles. She happily grabbed a handful of my hair.

"Better let me." Mrs. Anderson reached around me and ever so gently pushed me aside. I couldn't get pushed very far because my hair was still attached to Melody's fist.

Mrs. Anderson lifted Melody from her seat and stood by the side of the car hugging her. Her eyes were full of tears, and I thought she was going to break into wild sobs at any minute. Melody continued to teethe happily on my hair.

Absently Mrs. Anderson unwound Melody's fingers, and I was free. I followed the two of them into the house.

They went directly to Melody's room, and Mrs.

Anderson put the baby to bed—though I'd never seen a less-sleepy kid. I stood in the doorway and watched as Mrs. Anderson stood by the crib and cried.

Whatever's the matter, I thought, it's with Melody. I looked at the little girl happily cooing and laughing in her crib. What could possibly be wrong?

Mrs. Anderson walked slowly down the stairs, passing me but not seeing me.

I wanted to shout, "What's wrong?" But I didn't. She was so upset that I couldn't bother her. Instead I followed her into the kitchen, where she sank down at the table and buried her face in her hands.

She sat like that for a long time, an occasional sniff the only noise. Then she reached for the phone and dialed.

"Oh, Don," she said. "I'm so glad you're there! I didn't want to leave a message."

She was talking to Mr. Anderson in Boston.

"We went to see Dr. Linton, and Kay Mallin was there too. The tests came back positive. Oh, Don, she has it!" She began to cry, her heart breaking.

What? What does she have? I wanted to yell the

question, but my throat closed over the words. Melody—happy, wonderful, cute, funny Melody—was sick!

Mrs. Anderson nodded her head at the phone, her tears lessening. Whatever Mr. Anderson was saying was working.

"I'll look for you sometime this evening," she said and hung up.

It must be bad, I knew, if Mr. Anderson was coming home from his business trip early.

Mrs. Anderson got up and went to the sink. She turned the cold water on and splashed her face several times.

"Mrs. Anderson," I said hesitantly, "what's wrong?" I couldn't stand not knowing for another minute.

She turned slowly and leaned against the sink. "Oh, Charlie!" And she reached out to me.

I walked slowly towards her, and she took both of my hands in hers. She cleared her throat and opened her mouth, but no words came out.

"Melody's sick, isn't she?" I asked. My heart felt like a giant hand was squeezing it—sort of like I felt when Mom drove off with dumb Dink.

Mrs. Anderson nodded. "Very sick," she managed to whisper.

"But she looks so good!" I protested.

Mrs. Anderson pulled me to her and wrapped her arms around me.

It felt wonderful to be hugged because I was so afraid. I leaned against her and made myself ask, "What does she have? Cancer?" It was the worst thing I could think of.

"Worse," said Mrs. Anderson.

Worse? What was worse than cancer?

"Melody's HIV-positive."

I pulled back and stared at Mrs. Anderson. "She has AIDS? How can she have AIDS? She's a baby!"

"She doesn't have AIDS at this point," Mrs. Anderson said. "But she has the first step toward it. Sometime in the future, she'll have AIDS."

"You mean she's going to die?" I couldn't believe it! Melody couldn't die! I wouldn't let her!

Mrs. Anderson sighed wearily. "Eventually she'll die," she said, "unless someone finds a cure."

"But how could she get AIDS? She's just a baby!"I repeated. I remembered what they said on TV. You got AIDS from sex with an infected person or from sharing drug needles with an infected person. Melody never did either of those things. She couldn't even walk yet, for Pete's sake.

"Her mother's an intravenous drug user. She

must have had the virus and passed it to Melody even before she was born."

"But that's not fair!" I shouted.

"It's not," agreed Mrs. Anderson. "But life's not fair, Charlie. You know that from your own situation. You don't deserve a mother who takes off for California and leaves you behind, but that's what you've got. Melody doesn't deserve to be HIV-positive, but she is."

"How could God do this?" I asked. "How could He let something like this happen to an innocent little baby?"

"God never promises bad things won't happen, Charlie." Mrs. Anderson tilted my chin so she could look right into my eyes. "He just promises to love us through the bad things."

The phone rang, and I was glad. I didn't want to talk about God. I was too angry at Him to even want His love. I didn't think those feelings would make Mrs. Anderson happy, though, and she was already unhappy enough.

I could hear Melody cooing and gurgling as I went up the stairs. I went to her room and stood in the door watching her. She was lying on her back playing with her feet, pulling on her toes, grabbing them and trying to get them to her mouth.

I giggled at her in spite of my sorrow, and she heard me. She smiled and pushed herself into a sitting position. She held out her arms, and I went to her and picked her up.

We sat in the rocking chair, and I hugged her as she chewed contentedly on my hair. After a few minutes, her eyes began to get heavy. They'd close, and she'd force them to open. Then they'd close again. Finally she slept, and I cried.

I sat in my room for a long time after I put Melody in her crib. Half the time I lay on my bed and stared at the ceiling. Half the time I stared out the window.

Mrs. Anderson came to my room with a couple of Cokes. She gave me one and put a bag of pretzels on the bed beside me. She sat in my plump pink chair.

"We've got to talk, Charlie."

I nodded. "You're going to tell me that I can't stay here anymore. You'll have your hands full taking care of Melody, and I have to go." I couldn't look at her, so I took a big swig of soda. I could barely swallow around the lump in my throat. "It's okay," I lied. "I understand."

I did understand, sort of, but I didn't want to

leave. I just wanted to stay here and get hugged all the time, especially since I knew Mom wasn't making any plans to get me soon, if ever. And I'd miss Melody. She'd miss me, too. I mean, whose hair would she eat if I left?

"Oh, Charlie," said Mrs. Anderson, real concern in her voice. "You don't have to leave if you don't want to. Mrs. Mallin says it's up to you. If you want to stay, you're more than welcome! We want you to stay."

"Really?" I couldn't believe my ears.

"Really!"

We grinned at each other.

"Is it dangerous to be here now?" I asked. "Not that I want to go even if it is. I just want to know."

"Well, it's not dangerous if we're careful. The biggest concern for you would be if Melody bled. You must always remember that if she cuts herself or hurts herself and bleeds, you may not help her. You have to come and get me or Mr. Anderson no matter where you are or how bad her injury."

"Blood is the dangerous thing?"

"Blood is the dangerous thing. It carries the disease and passes the infection. Saliva has traces of the virus, but not enough to be concerned over. Other body fluids carry the virus too, but you don't need to worry about them."

"So I can hold her and play with her? She can keep on eating my hair?"

Mrs. Anderson gave me a big hug. "Yes, yes, and yes, Charlie. And I'm proud of you for caring about her so much."

I could get used to these compliments, I thought, even though I knew Mrs. Anderson gave them just to be polite. Mom didn't believe in giving them because she said I might become proud. Fat chance. Still, praise was nice to hear.

"Can we tell people about Melody being sick?" I asked. "She's not quarantined or anything, is she?"

"She's not quarantined, but we'll have to be careful when she's in public. I think we'll tell people on a need-to-know basis."

"Like who?"

"The people at church because she's in the nursery there."

I crunched a pretzel absently. "Will they let her stay with the other kids? What if she gets bopped on the head with a toy hammer and bleeds or something?"

Mrs. Anderson nodded. "Things like that are a real possibility. I don't think she can stay in the nursery."

"What'll you do with her during church?" I washed down the pretzel with a swallow of Coke.

"I guess she'll just sit with us in the back row. That way I can leave easily if she starts to cry or talk or something."

"The back row sounds fine to me," I said.

Mrs. Anderson smiled. "The sad thing is that some people will be scared, and they won't even want to be in the same church with her. It's important that we show her lots of love to help her get over the hurt others will give her—not because they don't like her, but because they're afraid."

We sat quietly for a few minutes, trying to imagine what the future would be like for Melody. The only noise was me crunching pretzels and swallowing Coke. Swallowing can be very noisy in a quiet room.

"I told God I didn't want to love Him or anybody," I said. "It hurts too much. But, well . . . now I love Melody, and it hurts, hurts, hurts." I looked away so Mrs. Anderson wouldn't see the tears in my eyes.

She nodded. "Love is risky that way. But do you wish you'd never met her?"

I shook my head. "She's too special to miss."

75

"Even though loving her is going to hurt for a long, long time?"

"Even though it's going to hurt for a long, long time."

"Charlie," said Mrs. Anderson, "you're a very special girl too." And she hugged me again.

We heard Melody gurgling to herself down the hall. "Let me change her," Mrs. Anderson said, "and then we have to go to the drugstore. I need some things for her care."

I stood in the door and watched Mrs. Anderson, wearing gloves like the ones doctors wear in the operating room, change Melody's diaper.

"See the rash on her bottom, Charlie? That's one of the things that caused us to wonder. It won't go away, and it should." Mrs. Anderson wrapped a fresh Huggies around Melody and carefully disposed of the old one, stripping off her gloves and throwing them in the plastic bag after the diaper. Then she sealed them both in.

"We're going to take what Dr. Linton calls universal precautions," Mrs. Anderson said as she pulled a one-piece outfit from a drawer and stuffed Melody into it. "I'll rinse out the tub with scalding water every time she takes a bath. I'll use gloves when I change her or care for her when she's sick.

Things like that. I'm glad you're older and can understand the dangers involved."

I had a new thought. "What about you? You've been taking care of her for a long time without any protection. That rash gets bloody sometimes, doesn't it?"

Mrs. Anderson nodded. "I have to have a blood test to make certain I'm okay."

The thought that Mrs. Anderson might be sick too was so scary that I pushed it from my mind.

"All because her mother was a druggie," I said, feeling a great rush of anger toward Melody's mom. "Why aren't all mothers like you?"

Mrs. Anderson smiled at me, tears in her eyes. "Thank you, Charlie. That may be one of the nicest compliments I've ever had."

I sat in the back seat with Melody as we drove to the drugstore. She stuffed great bunches of my hair in her mouth.

"How are you able to breathe through all that?" I asked her.

She drooled happily and grabbed my nose.

"You are a doll baby," I said, my heart full with love for her and at the same time breaking into a million pieces.

"Why don't you just stay here in the car and

keep an eye on the baby while I run into the store?" Mrs. Anderson said as she parked carefully between the yellow lines.

I nodded, wondering what I would do to keep Melody happy if she ever decided she didn't want to eat my hair. I hadn't been around babies very often since Mom disliked them so much, and I wasn't sure how to play with them.

"But I'll learn, sweetheart. I'll learn," I told Melody.

She grinned a toothless smile at me.

"When are you going to get some teeth?" I asked her. "Dentures must be a real mess to care for. It'd be easier if you grew your own."

She answered by grabbing more hair.

There were several cars in the parking lot, and suddenly I noticed Cheryl from the doctor's office pulling into a slot one row over. Then a big gray car pulled in facing us, blocking Cheryl from my view.

A horn honked, and both Melody and I looked around to see where the sound was coming from. A second beep, and I found the car. It was full of girls waving. I looked behind me to see who they were waving at, but there was no one there. I looked back and realized with a start that they were waving at me.

One leaned out a window and yelled, "Charlie!" It was Shannon.

I waved back. I started to get out of the car to go see what they wanted when Melody stopped me short with an abrupt pull of my hair.

"Good going, kid," I told her as I leaned over to unbuckle her. "I might have forgotten you."

Melody and I walked across the parking lot. I was careful, careful where I put every step. I didn't want to trip or something and cause Melody to get hurt and bleed.

"Hey, Sweet Stuff," said Shannon as she climbed out of the car and reached for Melody.

I didn't know what to do. Should I let Shannon hold her? If it was safe for me to hold her, then it must be safe for Shannon, right?

Melody solved my quandary by reaching for Shannon. Before I knew what happened, Shannon had the baby, and they were cooing at each other.

"Hey, Charlie!" It was Dee. She stuck her head out the window. "Ready for school tomorrow?"

I blinked. "Believe it or not, I forgot all about it," I said.

Dee laughed as though I'd said something clever. But I had forgotten. I glanced at Melody. I had more important things on my mind.

"Yo, kid! That hurts!" It was Shannon, trying to get her pony tail out of Melody's mouth.

"We've just been shopping," Dee said. "Shannon's mom and Cammi's mom work, so my mom took us all to Exton. Look! I got this great outfit. Don't you love it?"

She ripped open a bag and pulled out a bright purple top and a bright purple plaid skirt.

"Something tells me you like purple," I said.

"Does she ever," said Cammi. "She wanted me to get the same outfit."

I looked at Cammi's blond hair and pale skin and knew bright purple would eat her alive. Mom always told me that blonds should dress in light colors, and dark-haired people like Dee in bright colors like purple. "It doesn't matter what you wear, Charlie," she'd said. "Not much will help."

"Hi, Charlie." Mrs. Denning had a bag hanging from her arm. She reached around me and tossed it into the car. "Now we've got enough vitamins to last almost forever."

Shannon handed me Melody and climbed into the car after Mrs. Denning. Melody and I waved as they drove away. That is, Melody's hand flapped in the breeze as I made it go up and down.

"Good girl," I said. "What a good girl." I kissed

her cheek. She laughed and I kissed her again.

I didn't notice the car that had pulled alongside us until Cheryl jumped out. She grabbed Melody with one arm while she pushed me with the other. Then she hooked one foot behind my knees as she pushed, and I went down hard.

I ended up on the ground between two parked cars, stunned. My head rang from where I bumped it on a red convertible beside me as I fell, and then clonked it again on the macadam. Two lumps for the price of one.

I tried to get up, but everything started to spin as soon as I got to my knees. I discovered that you really do see stars when you bump your head hard—but it was one piece of information I would have been happier not knowing.

I kept expecting someone to come help me, but no one did. Hadn't anyone seen what happened? Hadn't anyone heard me scream?

I pulled myself erect by holding onto the convertible's door handle.

"Melody!" I cried. "Melody!"

But she was gone.

I limped into the drugstore, holding my head and dripping blood from the cuts I'd gotten when I fell in the stream at Hibernia Park. They'd been torn open by my fall, and blood gushed down my leg and over my foot, leaving strange marks behind me.

"Mrs. Anderson," I called as I searched the aisles for her. I knew I was weaving from side to side, but I couldn't walk in a straight line no matter how hard I tried. "Mrs. Anderson, where are you?"

A large man who worked for the store, probably scared by my wild appearance, came up to me at the same time that I spotted Mrs. Anderson.

"What's wrong?" he asked.

I looked at him and started to cry.

"Mrs. Anderson," I sobbed, stumbling up to her. "She took Melody!"

Mrs. Anderson's face lost all its color, and the man who had been worried about me quickly reached out to help her.

"Are you okay, lady?" he asked. Mrs. Anderson ignored him.

"Charlie, what are you saying?" she said.

I guess she couldn't believe what I said, but then I could hardly believe it myself.

"She grabbed Melody and knocked me down!" I

swiped at my tears. "She drove away with her! I'm sorry! I'm sorry!"

Mrs. Anderson took a deep breath and some of her color returned. She looked at the man and said, "Call the police. We have a kidnapping here."

The man stared at her as though he thought she was crazy. Kidnappings happened on TV or in mystery books. He looked from her to me, uncertain.

I nodded.

"Call the police," Mrs. Anderson said again, loudly and firmly.

The man still looked hesitant, but he did as he was told.

Mrs. Anderson turned to me and put her arms around me. "Are you all right, Charlie?"

"I don't know," I sobbed. "I bumped my head a couple of times when I fell, and it hurts, and I feel awful! Oh, Mrs. Anderson, I'm sorry!"

"It's not your fault, Charlie. It's not your fault at all."

"But I got Melody out of the car," I sobbed. "We went to talk with Shannon and Dee and Cammi. When we were walking back to the car, the Cheryl lady tripped me and grabbed Melody. It wouldn't have happened if we'd stayed in the car! It is my fault!"

"The Cheryl lady?" Mrs. Anderson looked totally lost.

But the next moment we heard sirens, and the police had arrived. I told them what happened. They were very nice to me and wrote everything down carefully. Then they sent us to the hospital with a police officer I found out was Cammi's mom. Imagine having a mom who is a cop!

The hospital people checked me to make sure I was all right. They cleaned up my leg cuts and wrapped enough bandages around them to wrap a mummy. They were especially concerned about the lumps on my head and took lots and lots of X-rays. I had a hard time lying still because I kept crying about Melody.

While we waited to find out what the X-rays said, Mrs. Reston asked me lots of questions. Mrs. Anderson sat beside me and held my hand.

"You're certain it was this woman named Cheryl?"

I nodded. "She was at the doctor's office this morning when we took Melody."

"What doctor?"

"Melody's doctor. Dr. Linton."

"Had you ever seen Cheryl before this morning?"

I shook my head. "But I saw her after."

"Where?" asked Mrs. Reston. She was so nice that it didn't seem like she was grilling me or anything.

"She drove behind us when we came home." I thought about that for a minute. "I guess they followed us on purpose, huh?"

"Who are 'they'?" Mrs. Reston asked.

"Cheryl and the young mom with the sick baby." I got excited. "I bet Dr. Linton knows her name and address. Maybe you can find Cheryl that way!"

Mrs. Reston smiled, patted my knee, and disappeared for a few minutes to call that information in.

"Is Cheryl Melody's mother?" I asked when she returned. "Is this a snatching?"

"Melody's mother's name is Sandy Elliot, and we don't think she's the woman you know as Cheryl. But we don't know who this Cheryl is."

I felt scared for Melody. "You'll find her before she has to be on one of those milk cartons or have-you-seen-this-child shows, won't you?"

"I certainly hope so, Charlie." Mrs. Reston patted my knee again. Adults seem to think that's especially comforting. "I certainly hope so."

The doctor came in then and told us that I had a very mild concussion.

"If you feel sick at your stomach or unusually sleepy, you tell your mother right away," he said.

I sure wasn't going to tell my mom, I thought, trying to ignore the catch under my heart. But I knew what he meant, so I just nodded.

Cammi's mom asked me more questions on the way back to the drugstore to get Mrs. Anderson's car.

"Did you ever see Cheryl again after the doctor's office?"

I started to shake my head when I remembered seeing her in the drugstore parking lot.

"I bet she followed us again!" I said.

"Could be," Officer Reston said. "Could be. What kind of a car was she driving?"

"I don't know. I don't know much about cars." I closed my eyes and tried to concentrate. "The car was blue and sort of little, and it had one of those backs that open."

"Like a station wagon or a hatchback?"

"A hatchback," I said. "A light blue hatchback. Of which there are probably millions, right?"

Mrs. Reston smiled. "How about the license number?"

I thought for a minute, then shook my head. "I haven't got the vaguest idea."

"Sometimes people put names on a car—the

name of the place they bought the car or a vanity plate with their own name or something."

I thought again but my mind was blank. "Maybe I could draw the car for you," I said. "I'm a pretty good artist."

Officer Reston looked interested. "You do that, Charlie. That might help us a lot."

"I might even be able to draw Cheryl," I said hesitantly.

"We ask eyewitnesses like you to work with a police artist to try and create a likeness of the criminal. If you can do it on your own, so much the better."

Mrs. Anderson and I drove home in silence. There wasn't anything to say.

They made me go to school.

"It's better than sitting around moping," said Mrs. Anderson.

That's what she thought.

"It'll keep your mind occupied," said Mr. Anderson.

Sure.

"It's always better to go to a new school on the first day," said Shannon.

First day, schmirst day.

"It's my first day too," said Dee. "Keep me company."

As though Shannon and Cammi wouldn't.

"Promise you'll call me if they find her?" I asked Mrs. Anderson as I walked out to get the school bus.

"I promise," she said. "If they do find her quickly, it'll be because of your drawings. As soon as I saw your picture of Cheryl, I remembered her sitting in Dr. Linton's office. But I couldn't have described her myself."

Mrs. Anderson gave me an especially big hug. I guess it was supposed to be doubly encouraging or something.

The school building looked pretty new and smelled of floor wax and Pine-Sol. Dee and I had to go to the office, and the principal took us to our classroom. Our teacher, Mrs. Something-or-other, gave me a seat next to Shannon, and I sat, a deaf, blind lump. I'm sure the teacher began to wonder if I wouldn't be better off in Special Ed.

At lunch I looked at the sandwich Mrs. Anderson had made me. Believe it or not, no one had ever made me a sandwich before. At home, I made Mom's.

I looked at that bologna and cheese on whole wheat and started to cry. Shannon was sitting next to me, and she patted me gently on the back.

"It'll be okay, Charlie," she said. "It'll be okay."

Dee was sitting across from me. "We're all praying for Melody," she said. "God'll take care of her. Here. Blow."

90

And she shoved a handful of tissues at me.

I thought the day would never end, but finally I was back on the school bus, staring out the window, wishing the driver, Mrs. Wu, would hurry up and get me home.

We drove through an older section of East Edge where the houses are joined together like old fashioned townhouses. The bus slowed to let off a whole bunch of kids, most of them pretty little. They lined up in the aisle and clambered down the steps, yelling and shoving the way little kids do.

Suddenly Mrs. Wu began blowing her horn and screaming, "Stop! Stop! Can't you see the flashing lights?" As we heard a sickening screech of brakes, she jumped out of her seat and raced down the steps.

All of us on the bus strained to see what was going on. There was a loud thud and the noise of breaking glass and a little kid screaming.

"Did somebody get hit?" I yelled.

"I don't think so," called Cammi, a couple of rows closer to the front. "I think the kid's scared, not hurt."

Mrs. Wu was scared too, and I could hear her yelling.

"Red lights!" she kept saying. "Flashing red

lights! They mean stop! You could have killed one of these kids! It's not like we're invisible, you know!"

I finally figured how to open the window beside my seat, and I stuck my head out. Mrs. Wu was standing beside a car whose front right side was resting against a fire hydrant. The headlight from that side of the car was smashed into sparkling pieces all over the ground.

Inside the car a woman sat with her head resting on the steering wheel. At first I thought she was hurt, but then I figured she was just thanking God she hadn't hit someone. A little kid in a car seat in the back was crying his head off. He didn't look hurt either, just scared.

Technically, the car had stopped before it got to the bus—thanks to the fire hydrant—so I guess it didn't break any law. All the little kids who had just gotten off the bus and several adults from the neighborhood stood around the car and watched as Mrs. Wu got the woman's name and address.

Suddenly it struck me—the car was a light blue hatchback. I looked at the baby. It was the kid with the bubbly nose from Dr. Linton's office. It was a different woman, but definitely the same kid.

"That's the car!" I screamed. "That's the baby!"

"That's Melody?" Shannon strained to see. "That's not Melody!"

"No, not Melody," I said. "The kid with the cold."

"What kid?" asked Dee. "What cold?"

"In the doctor's office with Cheryl. We've got to get hold of that lady!"

I rushed down the aisle just as Mrs. Wu closed the door and took her seat. I guess she didn't have to wait for the police or anything because there hadn't really been an accident.

"I've got to get off!" I was desperate.

"Sit down!" Mrs. Wu yelled as the bus began to move. She'd obviously had more than enough problems for one day, and it showed in her clipped voice. "You'll get off at your stop, and not before."

I sat because I recognized an immovable object. I waited.

"What are you going to do?" It was Shannon, whispering in my ear.

"I don't know, but I'll think of something. The first step is to get off at the next stop."

"Mrs. Wu will have a fit," Shannon warned.

"Tough," I said. "Melody's more important than Mrs. Wu's temper."

"Well, I'll come with you," said Shannon.

"Me, too," said Dee.

"Uh-oh." It was Cammi, looking torn. She took a deep breath. "Me, too." She made a face. Mom'll kill me. But it's okay." She took another deep breath. "I'll come. Dad'll kill me too. But it's okay. I'll come. I think."

"You guys are great!" I said. "Thanks!"

Mrs. Wu slowed for her next stop. The kids who lived there started filing off. The four of us waited until the last kid was starting down the steps, and then we ran like crazy. Mrs. Wu didn't realize what was happening until we were already out the door.

We could hear her yelling at us as we ran down the street. "Get back here! You can't get off here! I'll report you!"

Shannon and Dee had huge smiles on their faces as they ran, and Cammi kept saying, "I'm dead. I know it. I'm dead."

"What if she chases us?" asked Shannon.

"On foot? She can't," I said. "She can't leave a bus full of kids to come after us. She'll just turn our names in and never let us ride her bus again."

"Oh, boy," said Cammi. "I'm dead."

"What if she chases us in the bus?" asked Shannon.

"With all those kids still aboard?" I shook my

head. "She'd get into trouble if she carted them all over the place. She's got to stick to her route." I hoped I knew what I was talking about.

Up ahead we could see the blue car still resting on the fire hydrant. Its driver stood on the curb looking forlorn. Slowly she bent down and began picking up pieces of glass.

We slid to a halt beside the car.

"Can we help?" I asked. The four of us began to pick up pieces of glass.

"You weren't hurt, were you?" Dee looked very concerned.

The woman smiled weakly. "No, I'm fine. Just scared to death every time I think that I might have hit one of those kids. I just wasn't paying attention to where I was going. I didn't even see the flashing red lights until she blew the horn."

Shannon was peering into the car at the baby. "Is your baby all right? He's crying pretty hard."

The woman glanced at the kid. He was a mess. He was red and sweaty from crying, and his nose was running all the way to his chin.

"He's not my baby," she said. "I baby-sit for his mother."

"What's his name?" I asked. I noticed out of the corner of my eye that Cammi was writing down the license number of the car. A cop's kid if ever I saw one, even if she was scared.

"Brett Knowles," said the woman. "I watch him a few days a week while his mom works."

I saw Cammi carefully write the kid's name down.

"How do you spell Knowles?" she asked.

The lady answered automatically, "Silent K. N-O-W-L-E-S." Then she looked at us suspiciously. "Why do you want to know?"

"Just curious," Cammi said.

"What's your name?" asked Dee.

"Why are you asking all these questions?" asked the lady.

"Just curious," Dee said, trying to look innocent.

The lady snorted.

"Well?" Dee pressed.

"Mrs. Hoffman," she said grudgingly.

"Is this your car?" I asked. "Or does Brett's mom let you use hers?"

The woman narrowed her eyes at me. "It's mine. Why?"

I looked at the others for encouragement and took a deep breath. "Here goes," I whispered to Shannon. Then I turned back to Mrs. Hoffman. "Did you read in the paper today about the baby who was kidnapped?"

"The one with AIDS?" she asked.

I nodded. It didn't seem the time to point out that Melody didn't have AIDS but was only HIV-positive.

Now Mrs. Hoffman was really looking at me funny. "What's that baby got to do with anything?"

"The baby was driven away in your car," I said.

She looked the way I must have looked when Cheryl grabbed Melody out of my arms. "What?"

"Has anybody got a tissue?" asked Dee. "This baby's in bad shape. I used all mine on Charlie at lunch."

"There's a box on the front seat of the cover," said Mrs. Hoffman absently, her mind on what I had just told her.

Dee climbed into the car and began wiping the kid off.

Mrs. Hoffman said, "How do you know it was my car?"

"I'm Charlie Fowler, the one the baby was taken from," I said. "And I'm trying to find her and get her back!"

"Where does this kid live?" Shannon asked, pointing to the weepy Brett.

"You think Brett's mother took that baby?" Mrs. Hoffman's voice was full of doubt. "She can't even take care of this little guy. Why in the world would she steal another?"

I shook my head. "It wasn't the kid's mom," I said. "At least I don't think so. It was her friend—someone named Cheryl."

"Brett's mother is Chris." Mrs. Hoffman looked a little green as she said, "She borrowed my car yesterday to take Brett to the doctor's. She was supposed to bring it back before lunch, but I didn't get it until after dinner. She wouldn't say why she'd been so long. I tell you, if I didn't need this baby-sitting money, I'd quit in a minute. Chris is sort of strange, and so are her few friends that I've met."

"Did she ever talk about a friend named Cheryl?"

Mrs. Hoffman thought for a minute. "Never heard of a Cheryl," she said.

I was disappointed—I'd hoped we'd solve the whole crime on the spot. Still we now had valuable information we hadn't had fifteen minutes earlier.

"Where does Chris live?" I asked.

"245 South Fifth Avenue, second floor," Mrs. Hoffman said.

"That's only a couple of blocks from here," said Shannon excitedly.

"Here," I said, reaching out and pouring my collection of headlight glass into Mrs. Hoffman's hand.

Cammi and Shannon did the same. Dee climbed out of the back seat and added a collection of dirty tissues to the glass shards.

"Thanks for your help!" I called to Mrs. Hoffman, and we ran as fast as we could to Fifth Avenue.

"There!" shouted Cammi. She pointed to a large old house.

We gathered behind a tree across the street.

"What should we do?" Shannon asked. "Just go ring the doorbell and ask where Melody is?"

"Anybody have a better idea?" I asked.

"Well, there's one thing for certain," Shannon said to me. "You can't go to the door because Mrs. Knowles will recognize you."

"True," I said. "So who will go?"

"What should we do when we get there?" Dee's eyes sparkled with excitement. "Just ask where Melody is?"

"No. Too obvious." Shannon peeked around the tree at the house. "Second floor, huh? Let me go see if she's home."

"I'll come with you," Dee said.

Shannon shook her head. "Maybe we shouldn't let her see more than one of us."

Dee looked disappointed, but she agreed. "But I think we should move to a better hiding place than this tree. I'm sure we're sticking out all over the place."

We looked around and spotted a large rhododendron hedge two houses up the street. Looking both ways to see if anyone was watching, we dashed to our new hiding place. It was definitely better because it was so big and wide. We could all stand—except for Shannon who had to bend over because she's so tall—and watch number 245 without any trouble.

My heart was pounding when Shannon took off across the street, climbed the front steps, and rang the doorbell. We watched as someone came to the door.

"Who's she talking to?" I asked. "Can you see?"

"I can't tell," said Dee. "The sun's reflecting on the glass door, and I can't see anyone."

"Me either," said Cammi. She was biting her nails the way I'd attack an ice-cream cone.

Shannon nodded her head a couple of times at something the invisible person said, raised her hand to wave good-bye, and walked nonchalantly down the steps. Then she turned down the street away from us, crossed over at the next side street and disappeared from view.

"What's she doing?" asked Dee. "Where's she going?"

"She's leading anyone who's watching away from us," said Cammi. "She must watch a lot of cop shows on TV."

In a few minutes Shannon came slinking out from between the two houses behind us and joined us in the rhododendron.

"I cut back through the alley and a couple of yards," she explained. "I didn't want her to see you guys."

"So what happened?" we all said. "What did you say when she came to the door?"

"I asked her if she was interested in buying any Girl Scout cookies."

"In September?" Dee looked horrified. "Nobody sells Girl Scout cookies in September."

"That's just what she said. I told her I wasn't selling them now; I was just curious about whether she'd want some. After all, I didn't want to lie."

"What'd she say?" I asked.

"She'd love some." Shannon turned to Cammi.

"Make a note to hit Mrs. Knowles when the sale is on."

"Who cares about Girl Scout cookies?" I said. "What did she say about Melody?"

"I didn't have to ask. I could hear her."

I grabbed Shannon's arm. "Are you sure it was Melody? Did you see her?"

"I heard her," repeated Shannon. "She was crying fit to beat all. So I asked her if her baby was sick or just unhappy."

"What did she say?" I asked.

"Especially considering that her baby's in the back seat of Mrs. Hoffman's car a few blocks from here," said Dee.

My stomach was turning somersaults with excitement and tension as I waited for Shannon's answer.

"She said the baby was just sleepy, and she got cranky when she was sleepy."

"Mrs. Knowles said the baby was a she?" I asked.

Shannon nodded. "A couple of times."

"So how do you know for certain that the baby is Melody?" asked Cammi. "The evidence is all circumstantial so far. There are millions of female babies in the world, you know."

Shannon grinned. "Because Cheryl's there."

"What?" the three of us yelled at the same time.

"Cheryl's there?" I repeated. "Did you see her?"

Shannon shook her head. "I heard her. She started screaming at Melody to stop crying. 'You're getting on my nerves, kid!' she yelled. 'I've half a mind to give you back!' "

Cammi spit out a piece of fingernail and asked, "How do you know it was Cheryl shouting?"

"Because Mrs. Knowles—do you know, she looks like she's about twelve—"

"Who cares?!" I shouted.

"Calm down, Charlie," Dee said. "They'll hear us!"

I slapped my hands over my mouth.

"As I was saying," said Shannon, "I know because all of a sudden Mrs. Knowles turned around and yelled, 'Shut up, Cheryl! The kid's bad enough without you yelling your head off too!'"

"So Melody's really there," I said. I couldn't believe it. "Listen. I've got a plan. See that skateboard leaning against the steps across the street?"

They all looked where I pointed.

"We'll borrow it and here's what we'll do." I explained my idea.

Shannon nodded excitedly. "I can do that. No problem."

"And I can do my part," said Dee, rubbing her hands together. "I love stuff like this!"

"And I'm certainly good at crying," said Cammi. "Don't worry about me."

"Okay, then," I said. "Let's go."

"Wait a minute," said Dee. "Hands."

We looked at her. "What?"

"Hands," she repeated, extending hers. "Give me your hands."

We all reached out and clasped hands. I felt like an athlete before the big game. All we needed was a coach's rah-rah speech and a mighty group roar to scare the other team.

"Dear God," prayed Dee, "help us get Melody back safely. Please."

I jumped when she began to pray, jabbing myself on a particularly nasty rhododendron branch. Except for my week at Camp Harmony Hill, I'd never prayed much in my life and certainly never behind a rhododendron hedge. I looked around quickly, sort of embarrassed, but Cammi and Shannon didn't seem the least bit upset. I bowed my head then, but I couldn't close my eyes. It felt too strange. Still, I was glad that Dee had asked God to help us get Melody.

We were all set to move from our hiding place when there was sudden activity at 245. It was Cheryl, running to a tan car at the curb, suitcase in hand.

We watched Cheryl shove the suitcase in the trunk of the car and then run back into the house. "We've got to move fast!" I said and took off across the street. I cut between two houses up the street from 245, planning to sneak down the street through the backyards. My first problem was a high fence and the second was an angry sounding dog snarling behind it. Forget that plan.

I raced back out front, ran down the street past the house with the tall fence and dog, and cut into another backyard. This time there was no fence and no dog, only three little kids who took one look at me and started to scream.

"Shh!" I waved my hands at them, trying to quiet them. All we needed was for Mrs. Knowles or Cheryl to look out of a window to see why these kids were making so much noise.

The oldest of the three kids, who looked about five, threw a half-chewed apple at me and yelled, "Get out of our yard! Mom! There's a stranger in our yard!"

I don't know who was more surprised, the little boy or me, when the apple hit me in the back. At least they stopped screaming and started cheering. They figured they had driven me away.

I fought my way through a rose hedge, hoping Mrs. Anderson would consider rescuing Melody an acceptable reason to ruin my new clothes, and climbed a chain-link fence before I found myself in Mrs. Knowles's backyard. I pressed myself hard against the house and tiptoed around to the front. I had to let the girls know I was in place.

I had just raised my hand to wave to the rhododendron when the front door slammed and Cheryl came struggling down the steps with a shaggy car seat. I fell to the ground behind a scraggly yew bush and hoped my red shirt didn't show through.

"Don't help, Chris," Cheryl muttered to herself as she struggled to get the baby seat into the tan car. "Don't put yourself out for me. I wouldn't want you to feel you had to be nice or anything."

The door flew open again, and Chris Knowles

stood on the porch just above my head.

"Don't give me any of your guff, Cheryl. You just get out of here as fast as you can. The cops have already been here once because of you. Thankfully you were out getting that car and Melody was asleep. But I know they'll be back. I don't want them to find you, Melody, or that 'borrowed' car anywhere near my house. I'm in enough trouble already."

"Excuse me for living," said Cheryl. "But she's my niece!"

"I don't care who she is," spit Chris. "I can't believe you kidnapped her and stole your father's car!"

"Shut up, Chris! Do you want the neighbors calling the cops? Besides, I've only borrowed them." Cheryl stomped up the walk and brushed past Chris.

"I'm sure the cops will buy that line."

Cheryl didn't bother to answer.

"She's got AIDS!" hissed Chris. "You can't take care of a baby who's got AIDS!"

"I don't want to take care of her! I want to give her back to Sandy. She should be with her mother!"

"With Sandy? Hah!" The voices faded slowly as the two women went inside. "Sandy's so drugged up she doesn't know what day it is! I bet she doesn't even want Melody."

I stood up and waved like crazy. We were running out of time and fast.

Shannon, Dee, and Cammi burst from behind the rhododendron. Cammi grabbed the skateboard from the yard where it was lying and tucked it under her arm. The three of them raced toward 245.

When they reached the tan car out front, Shannon screamed and fell to the ground while Dee pounded on the side of the car a couple of times. Cammi dropped the skateboard just beyond Shannon, wheels up and spinning. Then she and Dee began to scream.

"Help! Help!" they yelled. "Shannon, are you all right?"

Dee ran to 245 and began pounding on the door. "Help!" she screamed. "It's Shannon!"

Cammi remained in the street, crying and biting her nails. "Is she dead? What'll we do? I think she's dead!"

Cheryl and Chris both came to the door.

"What's the matter?" asked Chris, obviously annoyed at being disturbed.

"It's Shannon," said Dee. "Look!"

She pointed to the street where Shannon lay

artfully crumpled, eyes closed, in front of the tan car.

"Help us," Dee pleaded. "Please help us!"

Cheering inside, I raced around back and up the back stairs to the second floor. I could hear Melody crying, and it broke my heart.

I grabbed the back door and pulled, but it was locked. I pulled again and rattled it a couple of times for good measure. Nothing.

I looked around frantically. There was a window just to the left of the door. I reached to open it only to find it was not only locked, but blocked by a refrigerator pushed up against it. I wasn't getting in the apartment that way.

There was one other window on the back wall, and it was even open. The trouble was that to get to it I would have to climb over the porch railing to a narrow, slanting strip of roof. I looked at the tiny collection of shingles that formed the roof ledge, then at the ground several feet below. A broken neck looked like a distinct possibility if I tried this trick.

Just then Melody had a coughing fit, the kind you get when you've been crying too long.

"Oh, you poor baby," I whispered, and over the railing I went. I got myself onto the little roof facing away from the house. Leaning my back against the house, I began to take little bitty steps toward the window.

It was a strange feeling to have my toes so much lower than my heels, and to have nothing to hold on to.

Oh, God, please don't let me fall, I prayed. *For Melody's sake.*

My right foot slid on the shingles, and I thought it was all over. But my new sneakers gripped before my foot went over the edge.

After a thousand years, I reached the window. The first thing I noticed was the screen. It covered the whole window, a big, old fashioned screen in a wooden frame. I stared at it in dismay. How would I ever get in?

God, please help me get Melody! Please!

Suddenly I noticed a tear in the screen in the bottom corner near me. Carefully, carefully, I squatted until I could reach the tear. I poked it with my finger. The screen was rotted with age, and it tore when I poked it. Smiling, I slowly stood again and reached out with one foot. I gave the screen a good kick with my heel right at the tear. The tear expanded. I kicked again and again. Soon the tear was large enough for me to squeeze through.

I ducked down and through the window, stepping onto the kitchen table. I accidentally kicked the sugar bowl, and it tumbled off the table with a crash.

I froze, waiting for Cheryl or Chris to rush out and grab me. I had no idea what they'd do to me, but I didn't want to find out.

I jumped down to the floor, slipping and almost falling in the sugar that had spilled all over the place. I grabbed the table and kept my balance. Then I went to the back door. I unlocked it and opened it wide. I wanted to be able to get out as fast as I could when the time came.

It was easy to find Melody. I just followed the crying.

When I walked into the room, I knew it must be runny-nosed Brett's room. Disney Babies hung on the wall and covered the crib sheets. A pile of stuffed animals filled one of those little net hammocks that you hang in a corner for just that reason. But I only noticed those things out of the corner of my eye.

Melody was what I really saw. The poor baby was lying in the crib sobbing her heart out.

"Shush, sweetie," I said as I reached over the rail for her. "It's okay. Charlie's here."

I picked her up and hugged her. She stopped

crying and began hiccuping. She grabbed a fistful of hair and rested her head on my shoulder. I melted with love for her.

I raced from the room. As I darted down the hall, I could hear Cheryl and Chris coming up the stairs, complaining all the way.

"So call the cops," said Cheryl. "Go ahead. What do I matter?"

"You want me to ignore that kid lying in the road?"

"Just wait a couple of minutes, okay? It's not like she's bleeding or anything. I'll get the baby and be gone."

"And how are you going to leave? Are you planning to drive right over her?"

Three cheers for Shannon, I thought. She was extra smart to lie in front of the car.

"I'll just back around her," said Cheryl, her disgust at Chris evident in her voice.

I hurried through the back door and down the stairs. Holding Melody as tightly as I could, I raced across the backyard. I was climbing the split-rail fence that separated 245 from the next house when Cheryl appeared on the porch, screaming her head off. I could hear her thundering down the steps after us.

I began running across the yard next door when a huge spray of water hit Melody and me. I gagged and spit and Melody cried out. The sprinkler ignored us and went on around its circle.

"It's okay, sweetie," I said. "It's only water."

I rushed across the yard, slipped on the wet grass, and went down on one knee. As I struggled to my feet, the sprinkler doused us again.

I glanced back, and there was Cheryl halfway over the fence. She hit the wet grass running and promptly fell. She hit the ground with a thud I felt all the way across the yard, landing on her elbow. The sprinkler washed over her as she lay there, making her language even more colorful than it already was.

I was over the fence on the other side of the yard and onto a brick patio before she was on her feet. I noticed her running awkwardly, her one arm holding the other. I was just thinking that a broken elbow probably served her right when I heard the scariest, deepest bark I'd ever heard in my life.

A gigantic, ugly dog loped up to Melody and me.

"Stay down!" I cried, hoping his wagging tail was telling the truth about his mood. "Look, Melody. See the giant doggie? He drools just like you!"

Melody stuck out a hand, and the slobbery thing

licked it—a difficult maneuver since he was wriggling on his tummy with delight at the unexpected company. The baby giggled.

"Give me that kid!" It was Cheryl, trying to climb the second part of the split-rail fence without the use of her one arm. She was so furious that her face was scarlet, making her look like a big radish with flyaway hair.

"Great and giant doggie," I said, "go say hello to that lady."

The animal grinned at Melody and me and lumbered off to greet Cheryl. He gave his loud bark, and Cheryl reversed directions so fast that she fell over backward.

I cut between the dog's house and its neighbor and ran out front.

Shannon was still lying in front of the tan car. Cammi was still crying, and Dee was banging on 245's door yelling, "Help us! Help us!"

"Yo!" I called.

Shannon heard me, raised her head, and looked. I waved my arm furiously.

"Yes!" she shouted triumphantly, jumping to her feet. "Time to go, Cammi. Come on, Dee!"

We raced to a drugstore on the corner, where we called the police. When we heard the sirens, we walked outside and watched a patrol car cut Cheryl off just as she tried to make her one-armed getaway in the tan car.

I hoped her father wouldn't mind the dented fender and broken headlight, but Cheryl didn't really want to stop. I also hoped he wouldn't mind visiting his daughter in jail.

I sat at the dinner table with Mr. and Mrs. Anderson and Melody. We were eating a pizza with everything except anchovies, but I noticed all of us big people were having a hard time chewing with our mouths closed because we kept smiling every time we looked at Melody in her high chair.

Mrs. Anderson had taken Melody to Dr. Linton as soon as the police brought the two of us home.

"She looks fine, but I've got to be certain," Mrs. Anderson said.

Dr. Linton had checked her very carefully. "She's A-okay," he'd said, smiling.

On the drive home, we had the car radio on. Suddenly it was talking about Melody and me and the girls.

"Kidnapped baby Melody Elliot, six months old

and HIV-positive, was dramatically rescued this afternoon by a group of fifth-grade girls led by Melody's foster sister Charlette Fowler, eleven. When the police arrived at the scene, Melody was already safe. The kidnapper, little Melody's aunt Shirley Elliot, nineteen, of East Edge, was trying to make her escape."

"Shirley?" I said. "Not Cheryl?"

We had almost finished our pizza when the doorbell rang. It was Cammi, Shannon, Dee, and Mrs. Reston.

"Mrs. Reston?" I asked before they were even in the door. "What's this Shirley stuff? Her name's Cheryl."

"It's Shirley," Cammi said, beating her mother to it. "But they call her Shirl, S-H-I-R-L. It sounds like Cheryl."

"We kept looking for someone in Melody's family or friends named Cheryl," said Mrs. Reston as she lifted Melody from her high chair. "It held us up for a while. We finally realized we were looking for Shirl when her father called to report his car stolen. He told us he suspected she had taken it against his wishes, and she needed to be taught a lesson."

"She'll learn one now," said Mr. Anderson.

"Kidnapping is serious stuff."

"So is breaking and entering," I said. "Right, Mrs. Reston?"

She had taken the four of us aside and lectured as sternly about how dangerous rescue operations were. Cammi had cried, and Shannon, Dee, and I had tried to look sorry.

"Obeying the law is better than breaking the law, even for a good cause," Mrs. Reston said as she took a glass of iced tea from Mrs. Anderson.

"But Shirl might have gotten away before you got there," I said. I never knew when to keep quiet.

"I know," Mrs. Reston said. "And you girls were wonderful. Just don't do it again!"

The adults settled at the table, drinking tall glasses of iced tea, with Melody bouncing on Mrs. Reston's lap. We girls went up to my room.

"This is such a pretty room, Charlie," said Dee. She pointed to the border of roses near the ceiling. "When we moved into our house, I had teddy bears dancing around my room. I hated them. Now I'm not so sure I want to get rid of them. They're kind of cute."

I looked at my rose-y room. It was amazing how much it felt like mine, even though I'd only been there such a short time.

God, I thought, *You're going to love me even if I'm not sure I want to love You, aren't You? I'm not used to being loved like that. But I'll try and get used to it. Okay?*

"Charlie," said Shannon, "we have a club called the Kids Care Club. We do little jobs for people, and we give some of the money we make to the church's Help Fund. We wondered if you'd like to join the three of us and Bethany and Alysha as a KC?"

"You want me to be in your club?" I was as surprised as I'd ever been in my life. I'd never been asked to be in a club before. "Me?"

The three of them nodded.

"You're sure?"

They nodded again.

"Wow! Yes!" And I couldn't stop smiling.

For more fun and adventure, read

The Secret of the Burning House

Did someone actually set the house fire across the street?

Dee Denning moves to East Edge, Pennsylvania determined to hate her new home. But the mysterious events happening to her new friend Cammi leave her little time to sulk. First, it's the Restons' house fire . . . next three of Cammi's valuable dolls disappear . . . then the family's picnic table is chopped into pieces!

Of course, the grown-ups at church are helping the Restons, but Dee wants to contribute herself—with money, that is. Just baby-sitting Cammi's doll collection and dog doesn't seem like enough. Dee's first job leads to the formation of the Kids Care Club . . . and to the solving of the Restons' mystery!

You'll find this and other East Edge Mysteries by GAYLE ROPER at your local Christian bookstore:

Chariot Books
David C. Cook Publishing Co.

Here's what girls like you are saying about the East Edge Mysteries!

"I love the suspense. I'd like to read more about Dee."
—Melissa, 12

"I like it that the girls are a normal group of girls. It is interesting to read about kids like you."—Kendra, 10

"The books are fast to read and you can finish them in a short time. That's just what I like."—Amy, 13